To Mami and Papi, who encouraged me to embrace all the colors of my story.
And to those who are just discovering new colors—and languages.

A. A.

For Grandpa Chelín and Grandma Jo, thank you for the color and love you brought to my life.

C. D.

SLEEPING BEAR PRESS™

2395 South Huron Parkway, Suite 200
Ann Arbor, MI 48104
www.sleepingbearpress.com

Printed and bound in the United States.

10 9 8 7 6 5 4 3 2 1

Library of Congress Cataloging-in-Publication Data

Names: Alessandri, Alexandra, author. | Dawson, Courtney, illustrator.
Title: Isabel and her colores go to school / written by Alexandra
Alessandri ; illustrated by Courtney Dawson.
Description: Ann Arbor, MI : Sleeping Bear Press, [2021] | Audience: Ages
4-8. | Text in English and Spanish. | Summary: "English just feels wrong to Isabel.
She prefers her native Spanish. As she prepares for a new school, she knows she's
going to have to learn. Her first day is uncomfortable, until she employs her crayons
and discovers there's more than one way to communicate with
new friends"—Provided by publisher.
Identifiers: LCCN 2021010660 | ISBN 9781534110632 (hardcover)
Subjects: CYAC: First day of school—Fiction. | Schools—Fiction. |
Language and languages—Fiction. | Communication—Fiction. |
Color—Fiction. | Friendship—Fiction. | Hispanic Americans—Fiction. |
Spanish language materials—Bilingual.
Classification: LCC PZ73 .A49135 2021 | DDC [E]—dc23
LC record available at https://lccn.loc.gov/2021010660

Isabel and Her COLORES Go to School

Written by
Alexandra Alessandri

Illustrated by
Courtney Dawson

PUBLISHED BY SLEEPING BEAR PRESS

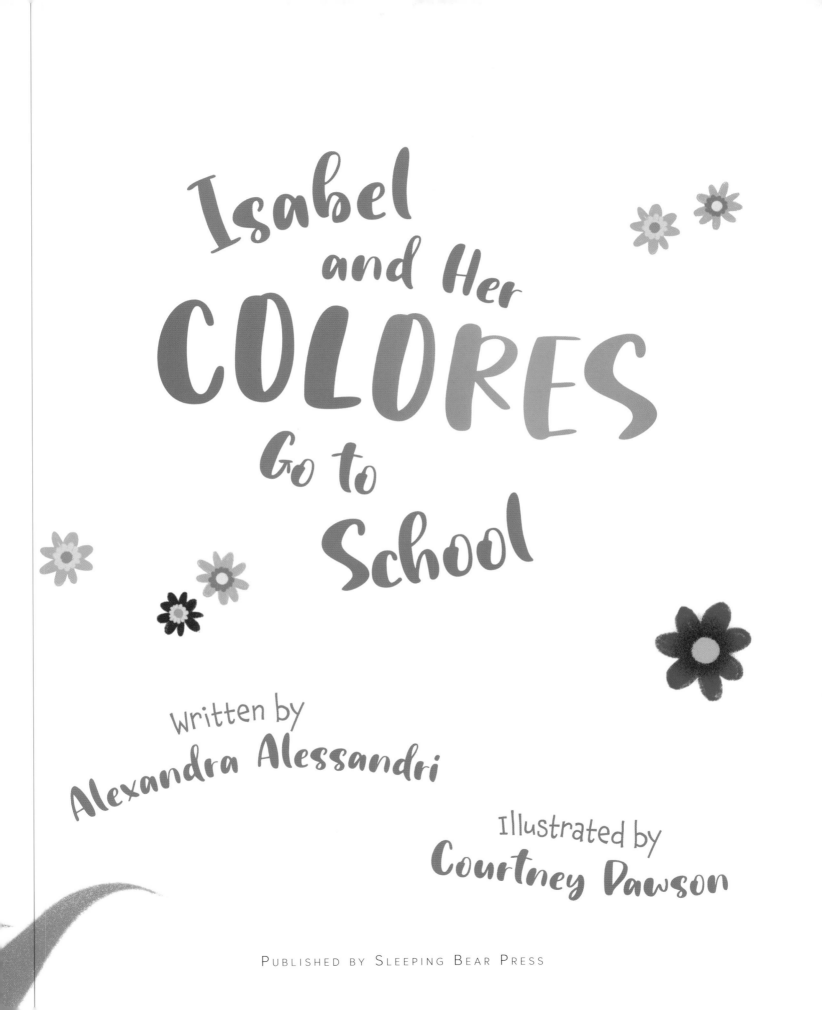

The night before the first day of school,
Isabel sat cross-legged on her bed,
coloreando with her favorite crayons:

rojo,

verde,

azul,

La noche antes de su primer día de escuela,
Isabel se sentó en su cama con las piernas cruzadas,
coloreando con sus crayones favoritos:
rojo, verde, azul, rosado, morado, violeta.

Estaba lista para las clases, solo que...

rosado, morado, violeta.

She was ready for class, except...

Isabel didn't speak much **inglés**.
English sounded wrong, like
stormy blues and blizzard whites.

Isabel preferred the pinks and
yellows and purples of **español**.

That night, Isabel dreamt
of all that could go wrong.

Isabel no hablaba mucho inglés.
Le sonaba raro, como
azules y blancos tempestuosos.
Ella prefería los rosados,
amarillos y morados del español.

Esa noche, Isabel soñó con todo lo que podría ir mal.

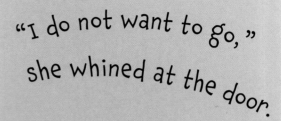

Cuando se despertó, Isabel corrió hacia mami.
Su corazón latía *tin, tin, tin* como lluvia de verano.
—No quiero ir—Isabel pataleó en la cocina.
—*I do not want to go*—se quejó desde la puerta.
—*Please*, por favor—rogó dentro del carro.

When Isabel awoke, she ran to Mami.

Her heart pitter-pattered like a summer's rain.

"**No quiero ir**," Isabel cried in the kitchen.

"I do not want to go,"
she whined at the door.

"Please, **por favor**," she begged in the car.

HONEYTREE ELEMENTARY

But it was too late.
They were already at school.

Pero era demasiado tarde.
Ya estaban en la escuela.

—Es normal tener miedo—dijo mami,
con su voz dulce y dorada como el mango maduro.
Ella le dio a Isabel un abrazo de oso.
—Al mal tiempo, buena cara.

"It's okay to be scared." Mami's voice was
soft and amber like a ripened mango.
She gave Isabel a squishy, squashy hug.

"Al mal tiempo, buena cara," Mami said.
"To bad times, a good face."

Isabel's lips wibbled and wobbled,
and her face tumbled down
into a tight, worried frown.

Los labios de Isabel
temblaban,

y su carita le cambió

hasta ponerse preocupada.

"Welcome," said Miss Page. **"¡Bienvenidos!"**

Isabel heard night-sky blue and sunrise-orange swirling around her.

—¡Bienvenidos!—dijo Miss Page—. *Welcome!*
A Isabel le sonó como si el azul oscuro de la noche y el anaranjado
de un amanecer estuviesen dando vueltas a su alrededor.

El sonido le recordó al café de mami, amargo y marrón.

The sound reminded her of Mami's **café**, bitter and brown.

When the morning bell rang, Miss Page
clap-clap-clapped her hands.
"Time for morning exercises!" she said.
Isabel wasn't sure what that meant.

Cuando sonó la campana de la mañana,
Miss Page aplaudió. ¡Plas, plas, plas!
—Es la hora del ejercicio—dijo.
Isabel no entendió.

But when everyone stood,
Isabel stood too.

When everyone stretched,
Isabel stretched too.

Pero cuando todos se pararon,
Isabel también se paró.
Cuando todos se estiraron,
Isabel también se estiró.

"One, two, three," the children counted.

"**Uno, dos, tres,**" Isabel echoed.

—One, two, three—los niños contaron.
—Uno, dos, tres—repitió Isabel.

She cringed at the colors crashing against each other,

like planets colliding in an explosion of stars.

Everyone stared.
Isabel flushed
cherry-tomato red.

Ella se encogió ante los colores, que se estrellaban como planetas chocando en una explosión de estrellas.

Todos la miraron.
Isabel se sonrojó como una cereza.

STORY TIME!

After morning exercises,
Miss Page wrote on the board: Story time!
Isabel watched as everyone settled on the rug.
She stood frozen. There was no room for her.

She felt as small and lost as a **colibrí** without its flowers.

Después de los ejercicios,
Miss Page escribió en la pizarra:
"Story time".
Todos se acomodaron en la alfombra,
menos Isabel. No había lugar para ella.
Isabel se sintió tan pequeña y perdida
como un colibrí sin sus flores.

"You can sit here," said a girl from the front.
Isabel knew what "here" meant, and it was enough.

—*You can sit here* —dijo una niña delante de ella.
Isabel sabía qué significaba "here" y fue suficiente.

—*Hi* —dijo la niña—. *I'm Sarah.*
Isabel sonrió tímidamente.
—Me llamo Isabel.
—***Want to be friends?***— preguntó Sarah.

"Hi," the girl said.
"I'm Sarah."

Isabel gave her a timid smile.
"**Me llamo** Isabel."

"Want to be friends?" Sarah asked.

Isabel shook her head
to clear the colors cluttering her head.
Her face warmed to a rosy guava pink.

"**No entiendo**," she whispered. She didn't understand.

Isabel sacudió su cabeza
para aclarar los colores que
ahí se acumulaban. Se le calentó
el rostro al color guayaba.

—No entiendo—susurró.

A Sarah le temblaron los labios.
A Isabel también.

Sarah's lip quivered.

So did Isabel's.

At lunchtime, Isabel sat by herself, doodling on her napkin.

She drew **corazones** and **caritas**, **culebras** and **carritos**.

Then she stopped. Even her crayons couldn't make her happy.

School was no fun at all.

A la hora de almuerzo, Isabel se sentó solita dibujando en su servilleta. Dibujó corazones y caritas, culebras y carritos. Pero ni sus crayones la podían contentar así que dejó de dibujar.

La escuela no era nada divertida.

Isabel trató de no llorar,
realmente lo intentó... pero las lágrimas
igual corrían por sus mejillas.

She tried to keep the tears in; she really did.
But they still dribbled down her cheeks.

De nuevo en su salón,
Miss Page cantó —*It's coloring time!*
Isabel se enderezó.
"*Coloring*" sonaba como "colorear".

Back in class, Miss Page sang, "It's coloring time!"
Isabel sat up straighter.
Coloring sounded very much like **colorear**.

And when Miss Page laid a sheet in front of her,
Isabel knew she had understood.

Y cuando Miss Page le dio una hoja en blanco,
Isabel entendió lo que tenía que hacer.

She drew
and colored
and painted.
She used
reds

and
greens
and
blues,

pinks
and
purples
and
violets.

Isabel dibujó y coloreó y pintó.
Usó rojos, verdes y azules,
rosados, morados y violetas.

She remembered what Mami said:

Al mal tiempo, buena cara.

Isabel drew the best two faces she could.
When she was done,
she held the paper up to Sarah.

Recordó lo que mami le
había dicho:
«Al mal tiempo, buena cara».

Entonces Isabel dibujó
las dos mejores caritas que pudo.
Cuando terminó,
le mostró a Sarah su papel.

—Amigas—dijo Isabel, señalando primero una imagen y luego la otra. En la cara de Sarah se dibujó una sonrisa. —Amigas—repitió Sarah—. *Friends*

"**Amigas**," Isabel said, pointing first at one image and then at the other.

Sarah's frown stretched into a smile. "**Amigas**," Sarah repeated. "Friends."

"**Sí.** Friends." Isabel giggled.
Sarah giggled too.

—*Sí. Friends*—Isabel se rio y Sarah también.

A Miss Page le gustó tanto el dibujo
de Isabel que se lo mostró a todos.
—¡Genial!
—¡Qué artista!
—Yo quiero dibujar así.

Miss Page loved Isabel's drawing so much,
she held it up for all to see.

"Awesome!"

"What an artist!"

"I want to draw like that."

Stormy blues and blizzard whites
softened to a brilliant **aguamarina**—just like home.
Maybe school wouldn't be so bad after all.

Los azules y blancos tempestuosos se convirtieron en una aguamarina brillante—como en casa—. Quizás la escuela iba a ser divertida después de todo.

SPANISH to ENGLISH

aguamarina:
aquamarine

carritos:
little carts

al mal tiempo, buena cara:
to bad times, a good face

colibrí:
hummingbird

amigas:
friends

coloreando:
coloring

azul:
blue

colorear:
to color

bienvenidos:
welcome

corazones:
hearts

café:
coffee

culebras:
snakes

caritas:
little faces

TRANSLATIONS

español:
Spanish

inglés:
English

me llamo:
my name is

morado:
purple

no entiendo:
I do not understand

no quiero ir:
I do not want to go

por favor:
please

 **rojo:**
red

rosado:
pink

sí:
yes

uno, dos, tres:
one, two, three

verde:
green

violeta:
violet